Dear mouse friends,
Welcome to the world of

Geronimo Stilton

THE RODENT'S GAZETTE
EDITORIAL STAFF

**Geronimo Stilton**
A learned and brainy
mouse; editor of
*The Rodent's Gazette*

**Thea Stilton**
Geronimo's sister and
special correspondent at
*The Rodent's Gazette*

**Trap Stilton**
An awful joker;
Geronimo's cousin and
owner of the store
Cheap Junk for Less

**Benjamin Stilton**
A sweet and loving
nine-year-old mouse;
Geronimo's favorite
nephew

# Geronimo Stilton

## RUN FOR THE HILLS, GERONIMO!

**Scholastic Inc.**

New York    Toronto    London    Auckland

Sydney    Mexico City    New Delhi    Hong Kong

No part of this book may be reproduced, stored in a retrieval system, or transmitted in any form or by any means, electronic, mechanical, photocopying, recording, or otherwise, without written permission from the copyright holder. For information regarding permission, please contact: Atlantyca S.p.A., Via Leopardi 8, 20123 Milan, Italy; e-mail foreignrights@atlantyca.it, www.atlantyca.com.

ISBN 978-0-545-33132-6

Copyright © 2009 by Edizioni Piemme S.p.A., Via Tiziano 32, 20145 Milan, Italy.

International Rights © Atlantyca S.p.A.

English translation © 2011 by Atlantyca S.p.A.

GERONIMO STILTON names, characters, and related indicia are copyright, trademark, and exclusive license of Atlantyca S.p.A. All rights reserved. The moral right of the author has been asserted.

Based on an original idea by Elisabetta Dami.

www.geronimostilton.com

Published by Scholastic Inc., 557 Broadway, New York, NY 10012. SCHOLASTIC and associated logos are trademarks and/or registered trademarks of Scholastic Inc.

*Stilton is the name of a famous English cheese. It is a registered trademark of the Stilton Cheese Makers' Association. For more information, go to www. stiltoncheese.com*

Text by Geronimo Stilton
Original title *Il tesoro delle colline nere*
Cover by Giuseppe Ferrario
Illustrations by WASABI! Studio (pencils) and Christian Aliprandi (color)
Graphics by Yuko Egusa

Special thanks to Beth Dunfey
Translated by Lidia Morson Tramontozzi
Interior design by Kay Petronio

12 11 10 9 8 7 6 5                    12 13 14 15 16/0

Printed in the U.S.A.                                  40
First printing, October 2011

# A Relaxing Vacation . . .

Everything was **READY**. Everything was perfectly **ORGANIZED**. I had planned it all down to the last whisker. Everything was in place for a very, veeeeery *relaxing* vacation. In fact, it was my first **real** vacation since . . . why, I don't even remember when!

Anyone who knows me knows I'm an **extremely** busy mouse. They also know I

Sigh!

love my job, even if I get **stressed** at times.

Oh, what do I do? Sorry, I almost forgot to tell you. My name is Stilton, *Geronimo Stilton*. I run a newspaper called **The Rodent's Gazette**. It's the most famouse paper on Mouse Island.

Okay, so what was I squeaking about?

Oh, yes, of course. I was going to tell you about that supposedly relaxing trip.

It started like this: I had decided to take a vacation. Nothing too exciting, you know. I just wanted to get away and put my paws up. So I headed for my trusted travel agency, **The Wander Rat**, to get some tips from Ms. Samantha Sweetpaws. She'd understand just what I had in mind.

Ms. Sweetpaws began leafing through some *pamphlets*, talking nonstop.

"Mr. Stilton, would trekking in the

Himalayas suit you? How about a tour of the Namibian **desert**? You know, with the lions?"

I had to bring her back to reality before she packed me off to the Roastedrat Volcano! "Actually, all I want to do on this vacation is **relax**," I explained.

"Squeak no more, Mr. Stilton!" she cried. "I know you well! What you want is an incredibly boring vacation!"

I blushed. "No, no, I'm not saying it has to be boring. I just want it to be relaxing."

"Relaxing, huh?" she chuckled. "Don't worry. I've got it all taken care of." She reached for the top of her bookcase. After a moment's rummaging, she removed a very large, dusty **BOX**. The label read **"Relaxing Vacations for Boring Mice**."

"But I'm not *BORING*!" I protested.

"Oh, please don't **lie** to me, Mr. Stilton," Ms. Sweetpaws replied. "I've known you for years. Besides, you shouldn't be ashamed of being boring." She tugged **playfully** at my whiskers. *Yee-ouch!*

Ms. Sweetpaws fumbled through the large, dusty **BOX**. Several minutes later, she triumphantly pulled out a tourist guide: *The Lazy Rat's Guide to the Black Hills.*

There were **PHOTOS** of luscious green forests, enchanted-looking lakes, and clear blue skies. Then a photo of the **Golden Dreams Hotel** caught my eye. The caption read "All-inclusive for a **super-relaxing** vacation."

**"Super-relaxing**?" I whispered. "Perfect! Ms.

RELAXING VACATIONS FOR BORING MICE

Sweetpaws, please book me fifteen days at the Golden Dreams Hotel and a round-trip ticket to South Dakota!"

Ms. Sweetpaws winked at me from behind her **GLASSES**. "Uh-huh. What was I just telling you?" she yelled. "You ARE a **BORING** mouse! But because you're such a good customer, I'll book you a first-class ticket, compliments of the agency!"

Ms. Sweetpaws spent a few minutes typing into her computer. "Okay, you're all set!" She gave me a free *tourist guide* and then gave my tail an affectionate (yet tear-inducing) yank. "Look at all the interesting things you can see in the **BLACK HILLS**!"

"Oh, thank you, Ms. Sweetpaws, but I don't want to do anything," I said, taking the pamphlet. "I just want to *curl* up in

## The Golden Dreams Hotel
### For a super-relaxing vacation!

Nestled in the heart of the Black Hills, the Golden Dreams Hotel provides all the comforts you need for complete relaxation and rest. We have large bedrooms, a heated swimming pool, and a gorgeous terrace with lounge chairs overlooking the park. It's everything you need for a super-relaxing vacation.

# WHAT TO VISIT IN THE BLACK HILLS

## Mount Rushmore

Mount Rushmore is one of the most famous monuments in the United States. It is carved with the faces of former presidents George Washington, Thomas Jefferson, Theodore Roosevelt, and Abraham Lincoln. More than 2.5 million people visit Mount Rushmore each year.

## Jewel Cave

Jewel Cave is currently the second-longest cave in the world, with over 152 miles mapped so far. The cave is composed of sparkling calcite crystals and other unusual formations. Exploring it is challenging but rewarding.

## Bison

South Dakota is home to herds of bison, also known as American buffalo. The bison was hunted to near extinction by settlers in the nineteenth century. Since then, it has been declared an endangered species. Now thousands live on federal lands.

## Devils Tower

Devils Tower is an igneous intrusion composed of many-sided rock columns. It rises majestically for 867 feet and is 5,112 feet above sea level. Its ancient Lakota name, Mato Tipila, means "Bear's Lodge."

## Harney Peak

Harney Peak is the highest mountain in South Dakota (7,242 feet). An old fire tower is perched at its summit.

one of those **cushy** lounge chairs with a good B🧀🧀K and **relax**."

I took my plane ticket. I was starting to feel *relaxed* already. I left the agency singing.

"Da, da, da, da, da dum . . .

this trip will relax me tremendously.

Da, da, da, dum!

Flying first-class will be just heavenly!"

# WHO? WHO?? WHOOOOOOO???

For the next few weeks, I was more stressed than a castaway on Tomcat Island. It felt like the day of my flight would never arrive, but it finally did. I hopped in a taxi and left for the *AIRPORT* in plenty of time.

I could hardly believe it was happening at last. I was going on vacation. A **real vacation**! And I was flying first-class . . . for free!

I headed for the check-in counter of the airline I was flying, **MouseAir**.

A plush red carpet led to first-class check-in. I stepped onto it nervously. Ah, it felt so soft beneath my paws! I scampered up to the counter like a **VIR** (Very Important Rodent).

Mice in line for the economy check-in counter stared at me curiously and whispered.

"Check out that mouse! He must be a **VIR**."

"Isn't that *Geronimo Stilton*? Look, he's flying first-class!"

The pretty mouse at the counter took my PASSPORT with a smile. She typed my name into the computer and stared at the screen. She glanced at me and then began banging at the keyboard, a *perplexed* expression

on her snout. After another moment, she squeaked, "Mr. Stilton, there is **NOTHING** booked in your name!"

"That's impossible!" I PROTESTED. "I booked my flight with **The Wander Rat**."

She nodded. "Yes, but your ticket was **CANCELED**. I'm sorry."

I stepped away from the counter and pulled out my cell phone to call Ms. Sweetpaws. That's when the pretty mouse **called**, "Mr.

Stilton, please wait a moment! Someone booked another ticket for you with **DIRT CHEAP AIRLINES**. Here it is!"

I took the *ticket*. It was made of a tattered piece of tissue!

I moved slowly away from the VIR window. I was totally mortified. I could hear all the mice around me whispering, "Isn't that *Geronimo Stilton*?"

"He's flying with Dirt Cheap Airlines?!?"

**"What a stingy mouse!"**

**"Who'd have known?"**

Dragging my suitcase behind me, I scrambled to catch my flight. As I scampered along, panting, I wondered: Who had canceled my first-class ticket?

Who?

Who??

WHOOOOOOO???

# A GARBAGE CAN WITH WINGS!

I boarded the plane and wedged myself next to a plump rodent wearing a **cowboy** hat pulled down over his eyes.

I settled in and tried to calm down. Once I got to the Black Hills, I would be able to enjoy my relaxing vacation.

No sooner had I finished that thought than the plane began to make a **TERRIFYING** noise.

I gulped and looked around. The airplane was in a state of total disrepair. The seat covers were **torn**, the *springs* had popped out of the cushions, the food tray wouldn't open, and the windows were **filthy**.

On top of all that, there was no life jacket under the seat. Instead, there was an empty box that said *You wanted to save a buck? Well,* **Too BAD FoR YoU!** *In case of emergency, you're on your own!*

I checked to see if there were any paper bags in case I started to get an **upset** tummy. Naturally, there wasn't a single one! Instead, there was a note: *You wanted to save a buck?* **Too BAD FoR YoU!** *In case of motion sickness, you're on your own!*

This wasn't a plane. It was a **garbage**

can with wings!

I looked up and saw the flight attendant **scowling** at me. "You weren't about to complain, were you?" she growled.

"N-no, everything is just **swell**!" I stammered.

The other passengers didn't seem to notice the plane's **shoddy** condition or the terrible sounds coming from its engine. They were all *SNOOZING*. Unbelievable!

The plane was speeding along, about to take off. I gulped and grabbed the armrests. One of them broke off in my paw. **EEEEK!** This was going to be a long, loooong flight.

Holey cheese, I was right about that. As soon as we were in the air, the rodent next to me took off his hat and shouted, "Surprise!"

It was my cousin **Trap**!

That was the signal to the other six passengers. They removed their **cowboy** hats, too, squeaking, "Surprise!"

It was my sister Thea; my friend Petunia Pretty Paws; her niece, Bugsy Wugsy; my nephew, Benjamin; my good friend Bruce Hyena; and my grandfather William Shortpaws!

I looked at them, **DUMBFOUNDED**. "Wh-wh-what are you doing here?"

Trap laughed smugly. "Hey, Germeister,

how do you like our little surprise? It's all my doing! When I heard you were leaving for a relaxing vacation all by your **LONESOME**, I canceled your ticket and booked a flight for all of us — on your dime, of course. Aren't you excited, cousinkins?"

Then he lowered his squeak. "This 'relaxation' is just a ruse, you see. You and I have a top secret mission: We're going to look for **treasure** in the Black Hills. But don't squeak a word to anyone about it!"

# DID YOU LIKE
# MY SURPRISE?

I was struck squeakless! When I finally found my voice, I stammered, "Y-you . . . y-you . . . y-you . . . did . . ."

Before I could finish my thought, the flight attendant interrupted. "Stop whining and sit down! We're about to start *rocking and rolling*!"

What? Dancing on an airplane? I assumed she was **kidding**, but at that moment, the plane started to go

UP and DOWN UP and DOWN UP and DOWN UP and DOWN UP and DOWN UP and DOWN UP and DOWN UP and DOWN

I could feel the cheddar croissant I'd had for breakfast rising in my throat. **Chewy cheese chunks!** I felt so sick I forgot to

ask Trap about the TREASURE in the Black Hills and why it was such a big secret!

As usual, Trap was as cool as cottage cheese. He never got sick! He settled into his seat and started leafing through a **catalog** he'd found in his seat pocket. I glanced over his shoulder. It seemed to advertise some very WEIRD stuff.

I was worried. What was my cousin up to?

I sighed. My tummy was doing too many somersaults for me to investigate now. But I knew I'd find out sooner or later.

# HERE, TAKE THE WHOLE THING!

The rest of the flight was painful, especially for my poor stomach. But luckily, the following morning we arrived **SAFE** and **SOUND** at the Rapid City airport in South Dakota. This was where our journey through the Black Hills would begin.

As we scampered off the plane, I realized I could **relax** at last. "By all that's cheesy

and delicious, we're here!" I shouted. "And, thank goodmouse, we're in one piece!" I was so relieved I *kissed* the ground.

My travel companions just **shook** their snouts. My sister mumbled, "That's my brother for you. What a **'fraidy mouse**!"

I didn't care. I was too **happy**. If I could **survive** that flight, I could survive anything — even a vacation with Trap!

I noticed my family members were all busy. It was great to travel with a *group of friends*. Everyone made himself **useful**.

Hello?

Yes, it's Thea Stilton!

I'll take care of the food.

Here, take this!

Trap put me in charge of renting the vehicles, since everything was on my dime.

The clerk from the rental car agency shook me from my thoughts. "Are you *Geronimo Stilton*?"

"Yes, that's me," I replied.

"May I please have your credit card?"

I gave him my MOUSE EXPRESS card. He swiped it, then looked at his computer screen and frowned. "I'm sorry, you're low on funds! Do you have another card?"

I gave him my MOUSE EXPRESS GOLD CARD.

I'll take care of the suitcases!

I'll buy the postcards!

I'm in charge here!

He shook his snout. "It's still not enough to pay for the rentals."

So I gave him my entire wallet with every **credit card** I had in it. "Here. Take the whole thing!"

The clerk took the cards, swiping one after the other. Soon there was a wad of receipts for me to *sign*. They were as thick as the last Ratty Potter book. Holey cheese! With all that money, I could have paid for ten relaxing vacations!

Trap was standing next to me. He didn't seem to notice the dent this trip was making in my wallet. He was too busy leafing through the *catalog* he'd found on the plane and squeaking away on his cell phone. Every so often, he glanced over at me.

Hello?

## I was worried. What was my cousin up to?

The clerk gave me back my wallet. I reached to take it, but it slipped out of my paw. All my credit cards **spilled** onto the floor.

Trap helped me pick them up, but I got the sense he was *smirking* behind his whiskers. He was planning something. I just knew it!

After he'd picked up the credit cards, he immediately started yammering on his **cell phone** again. He flipped furiously through the catalog.

## I was worried. What was my crafty cousin up to now?

Before I could ask, he snapped his phone shut and ran outside shouting, "Hooray! We're leeeeeeeeeeeeeaving!"

# WE RENTED

- **1 MOUSEBAGO CAMPER** with air-conditioning, GPS, electric windows, and automatic locks.

- **1 HARLEY-RATISON MOTOR-CYCLE** with a detachable sidecar.

- **8 MOUNTAIN BIKES** with sturdy and practical cushioned seats.

# ENOUGH, PLEASE! NO MORE SURPRISES!

Before we left, we had a delicious **breakfast**: bacon and eggs, pancakes, doughnuts, and orange juice. After the rubbery cheese we'd had on the plane, it really hit the spot. **Yum yum!**

We loaded the luggage and scurried aboard the **CAMPER**. Everyone, that is, except for Trap. He'd insisted I rent a **HARLEY-RATISON** motorcycle just for the two of us! He leaped onto the bike. I had to squeeze into the sidecar next to him.

As if that weren't bad enough, he forced me to wear a ridiculous leather jacket, complete with **fringe** and a bandanna.

"**Stilton family, let's roll!**" shouted Grandfather William. "We'll meet at Mount Rushmore. Last one there buys everyone dinner!"

With that, the camper sputtered to life and **sped** ahead of us. I couldn't believe a vehicle that big could go so fast! (Later Trap told me he'd requested the **SUPER-TURBO-EXTRA-VELOCITY** model. No wonder I had to use so many credit cards!)

Ready, Gerry Berry?

Uh, I guess so . . .

Trap put the pedal to the metal. The tires **SCREECHED** as the bike took off at breakneck speed. My stomach leaped up to my tonsils, then lunged down to my knees. *"ARGH! SLOW DOOOOOOOOOOOOOOOOOWN!"*

I'm not sure if my cousin didn't hear me or just didn't care. We kept **BURNING** rubber.

Desperate, I tried to distract myself from thoughts of being splattered on the highway.

Here we go!

Heeeeelp!

That's when I remembered something very important: Hadn't Trap said something about a **treasure**?

"By the way, what were you talking about on the plane?" I asked him.

"What?" he shouted.

It was so noisy on the open road, I had to **shout** to be heard. "WHAT WERE YOU TELLING ME ON THE PLANE?"

"SHUT YOUR TRAP, GERRY BERRY! DIDN'T I TELL YOU IT WAS A **SECRET**?" he hollered.

I rolled my eyes. As if anyone could hear us over the **SHRIEKING** of the motorcycle!

My cousin lowered his squeak. "Listen, the family vacation is just a DIVERSION. In reality, you and I are going to look for **treasure** in the **BLACK HILLS**! But remember, don't tell anybody. Not a soul!" he finished **MYSTERIOUSLY**.

I knew Trap well enough to be suspicious of his motives. "Could the **treasure** possibly be a secret because you don't want to share it with anyone?"

My cousin started making excuses. "Well, actually, we can't all **LOOK** for the treasure — we'd be too noticeable."

I knew what he was up to. So I decided that at the first opportunity, I would talk openly, **honestly**, and **TRUTHFULLY** in front of our friends and family about the treasure. I'd suggest we divide it equally among ourselves. But I didn't tell my cousin what I was thinking — I knew he'd just try to talk me out of it.

"How did you find out about this **treasure**?" I asked. "Is there a map?"

"We've got a lot more than that, Gerrykins!

You'll see. Not only do we have a **map**, but also an exp — nah, you'll find out soon enough. It'll be a **surprise**!"

Uh-oh. I was starting to get a bad feeling about this. Every time my cousin cooks up a surprise, it spells trouble for me!

"Another **surprise**?" I shouted. "No thank you! Stop! Stop the bike! I want to get off!" Trap suddenly veered onto a tiny side road that meandered into the WOODS.

Ow! Owwie ouch ouch ouchie!

We were bumping along a dirt road at top speed when he hit the brakes. "You want to get off? Go ahead!"

The next thing I knew, I was flying out of the sidecar.

"**AAAAAAHHHHHHHH!**"

*Squeak!*

I flipped through the air, head over paws, right into space!

I landed with a thud. Then I *rolled* down the path, banging my poor snout on every pebble and stone along the way. Every time I turned over, my tail was **CRUSHED** under me. I rubbed the top of my snout, grumbling. "I said I wanted to get off, not be thrown off!" I whimpered.

*Bang!*

Trap snickered. "Sorry, Germeister! You said to stop **immediately**. I was just trying to help!"

36

I raised my snout to the heavens in exasperation. That's when I saw a huge balloon floating above us.

It was a **HOT-AIR BALLOON**!

Two letters were written on it: **W.W.**

"Hey, **Gerry Berry**, do you like my **surprise**?" Trap cried. "See those letters, 'W.W.'? Do they ring a bell? I know what they stand for because, you know, I'm a genius! Besides, it was me who had the **brilliant** idea to arrange the whole thing! Wanna guess who's inside that hot-air balloon? Only the greatest **expert** on treasure in all of Mouse Island, that's who!"

Does 'W.W.' ring a bell?

# READY FOR ADVENTURE?

I squinted up at the hot-air balloon. I could just make out the outline of a **TALL**, athletic rodent. He wore a vest and a KHAKI shirt. But what was most noticeable was his wide-brimmed cowboy hat.

There was only one rodent in all of Mouse Island who wore that kind of hat. It was **Wild Willie**! Do you know him? He is a truly remarkable rodent! Wild Willie is one of Bruce Hyena's best buddies. They often travel together in search of treasure and lost civilizations.

Trap and I watched the hot-air balloon **descend**. As soon as it touched the ground, Wild Willie scrambled out and grinned at

# Wild Willie

⭐ **WHO HE IS:** An archeologist who loves adventure. He describes himself as a treasure hunter, but he doesn't care about money. In fact, he donates all the archeological treasures he discovers to New Mouse City's museum.

⭐ **HIS MOTTO:** "Ready for adventure?" If you answer yes, he'll reply, "Then go with the adventure!"

⭐ **HIS DREAM:** That mice will work together to make the world a better place. Wild Willie wants everyone to respect nature.

⭐ **HIS SECRET:** He keeps a photo of his girlfriend in his shirt pocket, next to his heart.

⭐ **HIS HOBBIES:** Studying ancient languages (such as Egyptian, Etruscan, and Mayan) and doing sports (his favorites are karate and mountain climbing).

me. "Stilton, are you ready for adventure?"

There was something about that grin that made me nervous. "Who, me? Adventure? What do you mean?" I blabbered. "No, I don't think so. I mean, definitely not . . ."

Wild Willie gave me a long, **probing** look. "You know, Stilton, I was surprised that a mouse like you would choose a **vacation** like this." He stroked his whiskers thoughtfully. "Aren't you a bit of a cheese potato? You know, one of those mice who's all about hot tubs, La-Z-Rat recliners, and all-you-can-eat buffets?"

Umm . . .

His words cut me right to the **tailbone**! I was so dismayed that I took my eye off my troublemaker cousin. It was only for a second, but that was just long enough for Trap to **TRIP** me. I shot up straight as an arrow — and landed right in the hot-air balloon!

I tried to scramble out, but my paw got stuck under all the supplies at the bottom of the basket. There would be no quick **getaway** for me. Trap had already hopped in after me, and Wild Willie was loosening the ropes that kept us tied to the ground. **"GO WITH THE ADVENTURE!"** he shouted.

With that, the hot-air balloon rose into the sky, **UP, UP** and **AWAY**.

I stuck my snout out of the balloon in horror. The ground was moving farther and farther away. "Help! Help! **I want to get out!**" I shouted.

Whiskers **flapping** in the wind, Wild Willie shouted back, "Too late! You can't get out now. But you'll like the ride. I give you my word!"

I tried to gather my courage. "**All right**, Trap, you've got me here. Now you owe it to me to tell me about this **treasure**!"

Trap put his paw under his shirt and retrieved what looked like a very **old** piece of paper. He shoved it under my snout.

The first thing I noticed was a terrible **STENCH**! The whole map smelled like rotten fish. **EWWW!**

It was a small, **CRUMPLED**, **TORN** sheet of paper. A piece at the very bottom was missing.

Here's the map!

Pee-yoo!

# TREASURE MAP

**IF IT'S TREASURE THAT YOU SEEK, LOOK DEEP INTO THE FOREFATHERS' EYES, AND DON'T FORGET TO PEEK!**

*The map was torn here...*

I sniffed and then almost gagged. "Trap, why does this map stink?"

"Because I found it at New Mouse City's docks. Someone threw it into a garbage can filled with **fish guts**," he explained.

I pinched my nostrils, took the map, and read the instructions out loud.

**If it's treasure that you seek,**
**Look deep into the**
**forefathers' eyes,**
**And don't forget to peek!**

"'Don't forget to peek.' I wonder what that means," I mused.

"I've got it!" Wild Willie **pointed to a spot** directly beneath us. "What do you use to peek?"

"Um, **GLASSES**?" I suggested.

"That's right!" exclaimed Willie. "So we

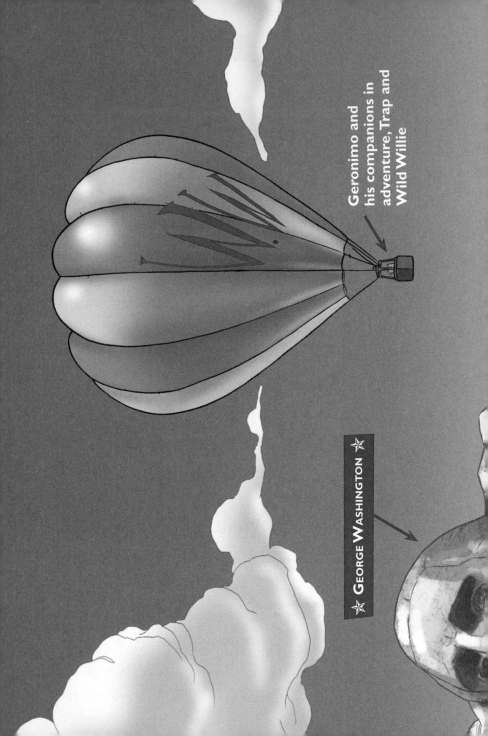

Geronimo and his companions in adventure, Trap and Wild Willie

GEORGE WASHINGTON

★ ABRAHAM LINCOLN ★

★ THEODORE ROOSEVELT ★

★ THOMAS JEFFERSON ★

## ★ MOUNT RUSHMORE ★

Mount Rushmore National Memorial is an enormous sculpture carved into the Black Hills of South Dakota. The sculpture shows the faces of four American presidents: George Washington, Thomas Jefferson, Theodore Roosevelt, and Abraham Lincoln. The artist Gutzon Borglum and his workers cut the giant heads into the side of Mount Rushmore from 1927 to 1941. Borglum died before the monument could be completed, and the work was finished by his son, Lincoln.

have to look there, from President Roosevelt's eyes. He's the only one wearing GLASSES!"

I followed his gaze and almost passed out from fright. We were floating above **MOUNT RUSHMORE**!

I slapped myself in the snout, then winced in agony. Of course! Why hadn't I thought of it? The American forefathers were the **presidents**! Wild Willie was a **GENIUS**!

"Great! But how are you and Trap going to get down there?" I asked **innocently**.

Wild Willie *twirled* his whiskers. He sized us up with his **piercing** blue eyes. "Well, I'm all muscle, and Trap is all fat, which makes you the LightesT. So you're it! Ready for adventure, Stilton?"

"What? Me! **NO WAY!**" I screeched.

The next thing I knew, they were lowering me out of the balloon.

"Go with the adventure, Stilton!" Wild Willie called down to me.

"Why, oh why do these things always happen to me?" I moaned. "For all the ⌂⍜⌰⟑⌇ in a slice of Swiss, I swear **ALL** I wanted was a relaxing vacation!"

There was absolutely nothing relaxing about hanging from a *rope* hundreds of feet above Mount Rushmore! In front of my snout loomed the faces of four famouse American presidents: George Washington, Thomas Jefferson, Theodore Roosevelt, and Abraham Lincoln. Their **EYES** were enormouse, looming before me like the **JAWS** of a pack of hungry cats.

As I dangled by my tail, I reflected on the fourteen years it had taken to carve Mount Rushmore. It must have taken tons of dynamite as well as the work of lots and lots of sculptors! What an **incredible** feat!

Then I recognized the giant features of Theodore Roosevelt and saw that he was indeed wearing glasses! **He** was definitely the one the map referred to.

I looked up at the balloon and shouted, "I found him! But I can't get any closer!"

"Try swinging yourself toward the glasses as hard as you can!" shouted Wild Willie. "And don't worry. If we think you're in **DANGER**, we'll tug at the rope three times."

I didn't want to, but I did as I was told. I took a deep breath.

Heeelp!

Hanging on to the rope, I began to swing and swing!
Hanging on to the rope, I began to swing and swing!
Hanging on to the rope, I began to swing and swing!
Hanging on to the rope, I began to swing and swing!

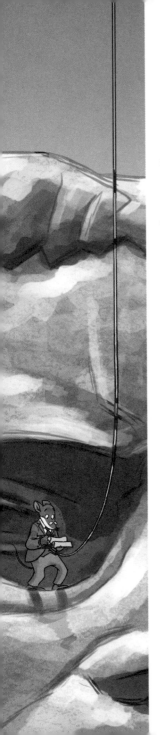

What a **cheese-curdling** experience! I was sure I'd be splattered all over the granite ROCK. Instead, on the very last swing, I catapulted myself into the dead center of Roosevelt's EYE. It was as empty as a cheese shop the day after Christmas.

Hidden in a corner I found a rolled-up piece of parchment paper. I pounced on it. Another clue! It read

**There are jewels that no mouse can part, These should be left within Earth's heart.**

# LAST ONE THERE
# PAYS THE BILL!

I slipped the scroll in my pocket. Suddenly, I felt three tugs. There was something **WRONG**! I pushed myself out of the president's eye and felt myself being **pulled** harder. The next thing I knew, I was dangling in midair like a rodent in a cat's claw! It was **TERRIFYING**.

I looked up, down, and all around. That's when I realized there was a crowd of rodents on the ground below me. They were all shouting and pointing at me. Petunia and Thea were among them.

"Look! Who's that rodent dressed in green?"

"Maybe he's a **FAMOUSE** actor!"

"Looks more like a complete **CHEESEBRAIN** to me!"

Then Thea shrieked, "Wait a minute, it's Gerry!"

"Impossible! He gets AIRSICK!" cried Petunia.

Before I could call to them, Trap and Wild Willie pulled me back into the hot-air balloon. Wild Willie steered the balloon to a clearing far from the *curious* eyes of our friends.

Wonder what it means!

Huh? I don't know! Hmmm...

HERE'S THE MYSTERIOUS MESSAGE WRITTEN ON THE PARCHMENT:

There are jewels that no mouse can part, These should be left within Earth's heart.

Somehow, he managed to land in the precise spot where we'd left the motorcycle and sidecar. We immediately began examining the **mysterious** scroll.

Trap took the parchment, held it up to the light, and turned it over. He inspected it for a long time, searching for a hidden **CLUE**.

Wild Willie was twirling his whiskers again. I could tell he was deep in thought. "Hmmm . . . inside Earth's **heart** . . . **jewels** . . . ," he murmured. "Stilton, give me your *guidebook*."

I handed him the pamphlet Ms. Sweetpaws had given me.

Wild Willie quickly paged through it. "Catapulting cowpokes, I think I've got it!" he declared. "We've got to go to **Jewel Cave**!"

I smacked my snout. (I really had to stop

doing that — **it hurt**!) "Of course! Jewel Cave! I read that inside it SPARKLES like semiprecious stones!"

Trap smirked at me. "Good for you, **Germeister**! You're almost semi-intelligent!"

Before I could respond, Wild Willie cried, "*WE'RE OFF*, Stilton! Adventure waits for no mouse!"

Wild Willie is a rodent of few words, but the ones he chooses leave their **MARK**!

You're right!

Let's hit the road, Stilton!

We're off!

Yikes!

Wild Willie and Trap hopped on the bike. Reluctantly, I squeezed myself into the sidecar. We burned **RUbbeR** as we *sped* toward Mount Rushmore.

Yes, you read correctly . . . we were headed back to Mount Rushmore, where I'd just made a **total cheesebrain** of myself. "I hope **nobody** recognizes me," I muttered.

Alas, my hopes were in vain. As soon as we pulled into the parking lot, rodents started pointing at me.

"Look! There he is," they **SNICKERED**.

"That's the crazy **cheesebrain** we saw hanging from the hot-air balloon!"

My fur turned **redder** than a tomato! Everyone was staring at me. On top of that, Grandfather, Bruce, Petunia, Thea, Benjamin, and Bugsy Wugsy had been waiting for us for hours, and they were quite **EXASPERATED**!

Petunia looked at me sternly. "Geronimo, I would never have expected this from you!"

"**Shame** on you, Gerry!" Thea shouted.

"**GRANDSON! WHY ARE YOU LATE?**

I've told you a hundred times: The early mouse gets

the cheese!" Grandfather William Shortpaws boomed. "That wasn't you hanging from a **hot-air balloon** like a world-class cheesebrain, was it?"

Bang!

I was about to confess the whole absurd story of the treasure and the **hot-air balloon**. But before I could open my mouth, Trap ELBOWED me hard. Then he kicked me in the **SHIN** for good measure!

"It's all Geronimo's fault!" Trap squeaked. "He got carsick—I mean, MOTORCYCLE sick! I had to drive **very, very slowly** and stop every two minutes so he didn't

Boom!

lose his cheese. You know how Geronimo is: He's such a wimp, and he's always *whining*."

I was about to protest when Petunia threw a paw around my shoulder. She looked very concerned. "*Oh, my poor little cheese dumpling!* How are you feeling?"

After that, I kept my snout shut. You see, I have a soft spot for Petunia, and I was ecstatic she was being so **kind** to me! Besides, once my friends spotted Wild Willie, they forgot all about me. They quickly **invited** him to join our group. Benjamin and Bugsy Wugsy asked for his autograph. They begged him to squeak at their school about his **archeological** finds. They even asked if he would teach them **KARATE**.

In all the **CONFUSION**, I didn't have time to tell the whole story, but I promised myself I would as soon as I could!

"Enough of all this chattering!" Grandfather shouted. "It's time to eat. I'm hungrier than a rodent on a **DIET**. Grandson, since you were the last to arrive, dinner is on you!"

# MAY THE BEST RODENT WIN!

Naturally, dinner cost me a **bundle**! We stopped at a restaurant we found along the highway. Everyone was so hungry they ordered **double** portions of the most expensive items on the menu.

While we waited for the **food** to be served, Bruce and Wild Willie stared each

other down, *grinning*. Without squeaking a word, the two friends rolled up their sleeves and began to **paw wrestle**.

"Show me what you can do, ol' Willie!" Bruce declared.

"You're in for it now, Bruce!" Wild Willie responded.

But the two mice were so well matched that neither was able to move the other's paw, not even by a millimeter! The wrestling match ended in a **draw**.

May the best ... ... rodent win!

Flashing a cocky grin, Wild Willie showed us a **scar** on his right paw. "You see this? I got it two years ago on an expedition to the Mayan pyramids. I came snout-to-snout with a mousetrap with razor-sharp **tips**!"

Bruce rolled up his pant leg and displayed a **scar** as long as a slice of Swiss. "Oh yeah? Well, look here! A starving **mountain lion** mistook me for breakfast!"

Benjamin encouraged me to join in the competition. "Come on, Uncle G, **squeak** something, too!"

Now, dear reader, I am a very quiet, **cautious** rodent. I spend most of my time at the office, glued to my desk. But I didn't want to disappoint my favorite nephew, so I muttered, "Oh yes, well, just look at this bruise on my chin! ① I got it from the **CORNER** of my desk. ② Here I **squished** my tail shut in a taxi door. ③ This one here on my right knee, that's from when I *SLIPPED* on a banana peel. ④ And this one came from slamming the refrigerator door on my paw!"

Not surprisingly, no one was impressed by my wounds. No one except Petunia, that is. She is always very concerned for my well-

being. "*Poor little cheese curl . . . he's always so distracted!*" she whispered.

Thea was less sympathetic. "That's so true, Petunia," she said. "My brother is a world-champion **KLUTZ**!"

Everyone chuckled under their whiskers. My fur turned **red** with embarrassment.

Bruce ignored my tale of woe completely. He was busy trying to impress Thea and Petunia. Using just one paw, he lifted a heavy **table** above his snout.

*Ehm!*

But Thea and Petunia scarcely noticed. In fact, they seemed a little **ANNOYED**. "I hope the **STEAKS** come soon or we'll have to watch these two compete all night long," my sister murmured.

Sure enough, Wild Willie lifted an enormouse **refrigerator** with one paw. Then Bruce grabbed me and began showing off a whole series of extremely *rapid* karate moves. He twirled me around in midair and, for the grand finale, slammed me on the floor like a wet mop.

They're so immature!

You squeaked it!

Then Wild Willie began his counterstrike. He IMMOBILIZED the adversary (me, of course!) by whacking me on the neck. So there I was, stuck on the floor, unable to move a whisker, until he finally relented and helped me up.

I scrambled to my paws, rubbing my neck. I was in agony! That's when I heard Thea whisper to Petunia, "I had no idea Wild Willie knew the secret art of karate's pressure points! Only a few masters in the world are familiar with that ancient Japanese technique." I could tell she was impressed.

Who knows how long this friendly (but painful) competition would have gone on if the waiter hadn't arrived with our steaks and the rest of our food? Thank goodmouse! Bruce and Wild Willie exchanged some heavy-duty slaps on the back and then shook paws.

Bruce picks up a
heavy table.

Wild Willie lifts
a refrigerator.

Bruce shows off a
series of karate moves.

Wild Willie immobilizes
me with a secret karate
maneuver.

"No one's **tougher** than you, Willie ol' pal!"

"Way to keep in shape, Bruce ol' buddy!"

Finally, we all sat down like a **normal** pack of mice and began to make plans for the following day. Trap immediately suggested we visit JEWEL CAVE. Everyone readily agreed that it was a very famouse cave worth seeing!

I opened my snout to tell everyone about the mysterious treasure. That's when Trap **PINCHED** my ear, **KICKED** my shin, and *smacked* me on the back. Before I knew what was happening, I found myself snoutdown in a bowl of cheese *soup*!

By the time I wiped my snout, Trap had changed the subject. Everyone was busy laughing uproariously at his impression of me with my snout in a bowl of soup.

I sighed. I promised myself I'd tell everyone the story of the mysterious treasure in the **BLACK HILLS** as soon as

I could. I was convinced that together we would easily find the **treasure**. And besides that, I wanted to divide it equally among us! My cousin Trap has a lot of good qualities, but when it comes to money, he's **GREEDIER** than my great-uncle Stingysnout.

After I cleaned my snout, I went to the cash register to pay the **BILL**. But when I looked for my **MOUSE EXPRESS GOLD CARD**, I couldn't find it anywhere.

Crusty kitty litter, I must have **LOST** it at the airport! What a **cat-astrophe**!

# Home on the Range

After I'd finally settled the bill, I followed my family into the parking lot. I found Grandfather William waiting **impatiently** behind the camper's steering wheel.

"Grandson!" he barked. "Would you pick up the pace?! You're **slower** than a slug at a snail wedding!"

My ears **BURNED** with embarrassment. I scrambled into Trap's sidecar. As soon as Wild Willie had climbed on the bike behind him, Trap took off in a cloud of dust.

I was **admiring** the landscape when Trap suddenly stopped the bike dead in its tracks. A herd of **buffalo** was crossing the road!

I was flung out of the sidecar. I landed within an inch of a buffalo's enormouse

horns. It stared at me **THREATENINGLY**, puffing hot, foul breath from its nostrils.

I tried to scamper away, but the buffalo head-butted me. The next thing I knew, I landed snoutfirst in a **pile** of dirt!

Unfortunately for me, it wasn't just a pile of dirt. It was the den of a big family of **prairie dogs**. The mother of the clan was not happy to see me. She chomped me right on the tip of my snout. Yikes! *That was a huge ouchie!*

I dragged my sorry tail back into the sidecar. I was so busy **massaging** my aching snout, I didn't see Trap's **SMACK** on the ear coming. "**Gerry Berry**, no need to show off," he told me.

"That's right," Thea called. "You don't have to pretend you can do **outrageous** stunts like Bruce and Wild Willie."

"Thundering cattails, I wasn't trying to show off," I screeched. "Oh, how did I end up here? All I wanted was a relaaaaaaaxing vacation!"

For the next few hours, we sat and watched the buffalo roam. Despite my aching snout, I had to admit it was an **incredible** sight.

When the bison had finally cleared the road, we resumed our journey. An hour later, we arrived at JEWEL CAVE.

I bet you can guess who had to pay the entrance fee for everybody. ME, of course! Trap made me choose the longest, most expensive tour: The Never-Ending Expedition.

The cashier looked at me, IMPRESSED. "Are you sure you want a ticket for The Never-Ending Expedition? Do you understand why it's called that?"

I felt my knees quake with fright. I was about to give back the tickets when Trap grabbed them. "I'll take those, thank you!"

We put on speleologists'* helmets and rain gear and followed our guide. She led us through broad caves with walls covered by minerals that shone like jewels. Calcites hung from all sides. It was amazing!

Suddenly, our guide turned down a small, dark, NARROW, and very muddy tunnel.

"Snouts up, rodents. The fun begins now!" Bruce exclaimed.

Wild Willie winked at me, twirling his whiskers. "Ready for adventure, Stilton?"

"Of course he's ready!" Trap answered for me. He shoved me ahead of him down the dark, narrow tunnel. For a moment, I felt nothing under my paws but EMPTY air!

So began my reckless descent down a

*Speleologist: A scholar and explorer of underground caves

**long**, dark, slippery tunnel. I went dOWN, dOWN, **down**. And I was completely alone. My friends had disappeared!

At last, my paws splashed into a pool of CLEAR, **freezing** water. As the light of my helmet glinted across the water, I noticed the pool was in the shape of a **heart**.

A heart? That reminded me of something. Suddenly, the words of the last clue came back to me:

There are jewels that no mouse can part,

These should be left within Earth's heart.

I dove down into the frozen water. At the bottom of the **heart-shaped** pool I saw writing. Tiny quartz PEBBLES that shone like jewels spelled a message:

On the Black Hills' highest crest,

You will find the key to the treasure.

Giddyup now, if you know what's best —

Or you'll lose by any measure!

I emerged from the frozen water, repeating the *message* so I wouldn't forget it. This was the clue that could lead us to the treasure in the Black Hills! Yee-haw!

But after a moment, I started to panic. I'd almost forgotten I had a **BIG** problem: I was lost in a **deep, dark** cave, hundreds of feet beneath the earth!

Terrified, I yelled, "HEEEELP! HEEEELP!"

# BEWARE OF THE
# MOUNTAIN LION!

I immediately heard a familiar **SQUEAK**.
"Take it easy, champ," the voice said.
"Just stick with me and we'll slide out
of here quicker than an *earthworm*
slides through mud!"

It was Bruce! I grabbed his paw, and
together we scampered through **dark tunnel**
after **dark tunnel**.

When we finally reached
**DAYLIGHT**, I was covered
in mud, just like an
earthworm! Before I passed
out, I managed to murmur,
"Clue . . . treasure . . .
Black Hills . . ."

Bruce and Wild Willie carried me to the camper and put me to bed with a **HOT WATER** bottle on my paws. I had a *fever* and a pretty bad cold!

Between sneezes, I told everyone the truth about Trap's **MYstERIOUs** map and the search for treasure in the Black Hills. Then I revealed what I had read at the bottom of the heart-shaped pool.

"The pebbles spelled:

**On the Black Hills' highest crest,**
**You will find the key to the treasure.**
**Giddyup now, if you know what's best —**
**Or you'll lose by any measure!**

"Hmm," said Wild Willie. "The highest point of the Black Hills is Harney Peak, at 7,242 feet!"

"Great! We'll **CLIMB** it tomorrow at dawn!" declared Bruce.

"Cheese niblets!" exclaimed Benjamin and Bugsy Wugsy. "We're going treasure hunting!"

"Yeah, for MY treasure!" whined Trap.

I smiled. I knew I was too sick for Trap to get mad at me. "Our treasure . . . We'll search for it together, we'll find it together, and we'll divide it among ourselves together! That's what friends do!"

Before we went to bed, Wild Willie and

## ☆ Harney Peak ☆

Harney Peak is the highest point in South Dakota. It is also the highest summit in the United States east of the Rocky Mountains. At the top of the peak, there's an old stone tower. The place was named for General William S. Harney during the 1850s. Harney Peak is located in the Black Elk Wilderness, named for the Lakota (Sioux) chief Black Elk, who experienced a great vision there.

Bruce called us together for last-minute instructions. Bruce was the first to squeak.

"Do you remember the **mountain lion** that took a **bite** out of my back leg? It happened right around here!"

We all looked at each other nervously.

"When we go out tomorrow, keep together as a group and stick to the path!" Wild Willie continued. "If you come **SNOUT-to-SNOUt** with a mountain lion, don't scurry away. Stare him in the **EYES**, or he'll smell your fear and **ATTACK** you!"

"Never turn your back on the mountain lion, and don't bend down. He could mistake you for **pREY**!" Bruce added. "Try to look as big as you can, and slowly back away. Move your paws up and down. If the mountain lion seems aggressive, throw **ROCKS** or **branches** at him!"

# TWO TERRIBLE YELLOW EYES . . .

I couldn't sleep that night. I tossed and turned, dreaming a hungry mountain lion was at my heels. It was terrifying!

At dawn the next day, I was pooped before we even began climbing Harney Peak. My fur was as PALE as a slice of mozzarella. "Go on ahead. I'm staying here," I told my friends. "I can't move another inch! I'm too AFRAID of mountain lions."

Trap rubbed his paws together eagerly. "Have it your way, Gerrykins. That makes one less rodent to share the treasure with."

"MOUSE UP, Gerry!" Thea demanded. "For once in your life, don't be such a SCAREDY-RAT!"

Grandfather William agreed. "Grandson, a true Stilton never gives up!" he thundered.

Wild Willie looked at me. "Stilton, yesterday you told me you were **ready** for adventure!"

"Yes, but that was before anyone said anything about **mountain lions**!" I pointed out.

"It wouldn't be an adventure without a whiff of danger!" Wild Willie responded.

"That's right, cheese puff!" Bruce exclaimed. "You can do this!"

"Come on, Uncle G. If we stay together, nothing bad will happen to us!" Benjamin said. "Besides, think of the **treasure**!"

Petunia came and put her **paw** around me. "Geronimo, I know you have the **COURAGE** to do this. Let's go!"

I had no choice. They were all against me.

Foolishly, I let myself be convinced.

I followed Bruce and Wild Willie down the path leading toward the forest. We hiked along at a brisk pace. I had to stop to catch my breath every so often. Every time I slowed down, the **distance** between me and the others grew wider.

For an instant, I lost sight of them altogether. I heard Bruce hollering at me from up ahead. "Come on, champ! *MOVE THAT TAIL!*"

Only Bugsy Wugsy stayed at my side to keep me company. She wasn't tired; she just felt sorry for me. She was a *kindhearted* little rodent, just like her aunt Petunia.

After a little while, I had to stop and sit down. I couldn't move another inch!

Bugsy Wugsy started chasing *butterflies* while I rummaged

through my backpack in search of an energy **BAR**, a piece of cheese — anything that would give me some **STRENGTH**. "Aha!" I cried, pulling out a piece of **CHOCOLATE**. I turned to offer a piece to Bugsy Wugsy, but . . .

## She had disappeared!

Then I heard a scream.

I looked around frantically. Where was she?

At last I saw her. Bugsy Wugsy had slipped and was dangling by her shirt from a branch on a large tree trunk. The trunk was stretched across a deep gorge. She was literally hanging by a thread!

At the other end of the trunk was an enormouse **mountain lion**, sitting very still, staring at her! That bloodthirsty feline was licking his whiskers in anticipation of a delicious meal.

There was no time to lose. I grabbed a **branch**. I stepped onto the trunk and glanced down. EMPTY air loomed below me. Determined not to fall, I tried to fix my eyes on something in front of me. To my **horror**, I found I was eyeball-to-eyeball with the ferocious mountain lion!

I advanced slowly. With the help of the branch, I was able to keep my balance — until one of my **PAWS** slipped! I screamed and waved the branch like a madmouse, trying desperately to hold on. "**HEEEEEELP!**"

I slipped and fell to the bottom of the gorge. The last thing I saw was the mountain lion running away, wagging its tail behind it. I was puzzled until I realized my **HYSTERICS** had frightened it away!

After that, I blacked out.

# THE KEY TO THE TREASURE

When I came to, the first things I saw were . . . Petunia's **blue** eyes.

I sighed. Then I remembered Bugsy Wugsy! Was she okay? I looked around in panic. Yes, she was still in one piece. I sighed with relief.

Wild Willie slapped me on the shoulder. "WELL DONE, Stilton. You remembered what to do when facing a mountain lion."

Bruce slapped my other shoulder. I winced. "Champ, on those rare occasions when you don't disappoint me, you do me **PROUD**!"

Petunia gave me a kiss on the tip of my snout. "Gerry, you're a real hero!"

Trap just shouted, "Germeister, your little **RatNaP** is over. Get up and let's find the treasure before somebody else does!"

I gulped. "Do we have to climb Harney Peak again? It'll take **FOREVER**!"

"Not to worry, Gerrykins," Thea said. "While you were out cold, we scaled Harney Peak and found this **key**."

Trap showed me an old key and an ancient parchment with this message on it:

Benjamin was so excited he was bouncing up and down. "**HOLEY CHEESE**, there's really a **treasure**!"

At the foot of Bear's Lodge, you will find the gold . . . Seek it there, if you will be so bold!

"Where is **BEAR'S LODGE**?" asked Bugsy Wugsy.

A lightbulb went on in my head. I began

leafing through my guidebook. "Bear's Lodge is also called Devils Tower! It's a tall, **RUGGED** rock that looks like a tower, and it's in the northeastern part of Wyoming!"

"Well then, rodents, let's saddle up!" Trap cried. "The treasure won't wait forever!"

We got to Devils Tower in record time. As we pulled into the parking lot, we found a surprise: an immense **crowd**.

There was also a **band**, complete with trumpets and drums!

"Wh-why are all these rodents here?" I stammered.

At the front of the crowd was a stand festooned with ribbons. A rodent standing on top shouted into a **megaphone**. "This year, the treasure hunt was a real success. Over a thousand rodents signed up. With the money we raised from their fees, we'll

## ☆ Devils Tower ☆

Devils Tower is a steep, rugged, solitary stump-shaped rock that looms 1,267 feet over the Belle Fourche River below. It is 867 feet from its base to its summit. Located in northeastern Wyoming, Devils Tower formed from magma that swelled into the sedimentary rock around it. The sedimentary rock eventually eroded, leaving the unusual structure that remains. Also known as Bear's Lodge, or Mato Tipila, Devils Tower is a sacred site to many Native Americans. It was declared America's first national monument by Theodore Roosevelt in 1906.

be able to protect *nature* in the Black Hills! So let me present the winners of this year's **Black Hills Treasure Hunt Benefit!**"

Treasure hunt . . . benefit? We all looked at one another in **shock**. We had been participating in a contest this whole time?

Before we could react, the crowd cheered **enthusiastically** and pushed us onto the stand.

The rodent with the megaphone shouted, "Now for the moment you've been waiting for — the presentation of the treasure!"

He asked us to give him the **key** we had found. Thea gave it to him. He inserted it into the lock of a wooden chest and opened it.

It was filled with **golden coins**! Trap reached in with both paws and showered coins over his snout. "**I'M RICH!**"

The crowd was silent. Everyone stared at him in ASTONISHMENT.

The rodent on the podium was confused.

"RICH? But this isn't **real** gold."

"Wh-what?! Wait a minute, what are these?" screeched Trap. He sniffed one of the coins. "B-but . . . these are made of **chocolate**!"

The rodent smiled. "Yes, of course. You see, the prize is just *symbolic*. The real prize is participating, because the real treasure is nature! That's why we organized this whole **CONTEST** — to raise money to preserve the natural beauty of the Black Hills."

He waved a **flyer** under our snouts. It was an exact copy of the "map" Trap had found, complete with the missing **PIECE**!

We were all squeakless.

Wild Willie winked at me. "Trap, I have a **confession** to make. I knew this was a **fund-raiser**. In fact, I paid the entrance fee for everybody in our group.

**IF IT'S TREASURE THAT YOU SEEK,
LOOK DEEP INTO THE FOREFATHERS'
EYES, AND DON'T FORGET TO PEEK!**

**HELP PRESERVE THE BLACK HILLS'
NATURAL BEAUTY! FOLLOW THE CLUES
AND FIND THE TREASURE!**

### RULES OF THE GAME

We've organized this treasure hunt to raise
money to preserve nature in the Black Hills.
The team that finishes first will receive a prize
of real coins made of . . . pure chocolate! All
proceeds from the contest's entrance fee will go
to the Black Hills Nature Society.

 **NATURE IS THE MOST PRECIOUS TREASURE!** ❋

I wanted to give you all a present: an amazing **ADVENTURE**!"

Trap shrieked and tore at his fur. "**NOOOOO!** It's not fair! I wanted a **REAL** treasure!"

My fur turned bright red. Trap could be so **embarrassing**!

"Ha-ha, that's Trap for you!" I told the crowd. "He's such a jokester! We are very **happy** we could participate in this magnificent adventure!"

NATURE IS THE MOST PRECIOUS TREASURE!

# I'll Give You a
# Mountain Lion!

After that, we headed home to New
Mouse City. I reflected that the vacation
was certainly not a relaxing one, but
it was without doubt one of the most
beautiful trips of my life!

I turned toward Trap, who was sitting
next to me. He was comforting himself by
EATING the chocolate coins.

"Thank you, Trap," I said. "Because
of you, I had a *wonderful*
time!"

"Well, I wouldn't thank me
just yet," he said mischievously.
"I have one last **surprise** for
you, Ger!"

What **surprise** did my cousin have planned this time? I was afraid to find out!

When we landed in New Mouse City, I headed straight to my apartment at 8 Mouseford Lane with Trap right behind me. A **HUGE** pile of packages was waiting for me there!

Trap shouted, **"Do you like your surprise, Germeister?** I ordered all these neat little things from the catalog I found on the plane. **Naturally, you're paying the bill.** I ordered everything with this!"

And he waved my **MOUSE EXPRESS GOLD CARD** in front of my snout. It was the card I thought I'd lost at the beginning of our trip!

I glanced at the pile of things.

"Wh-what? A ***mountain lion***?" I squeaked in horror.

Yep, right on top of the pile of boxes was a mountain lion. It looked as if it was about to **POUNCE** on me.

I stared it in the eye for a moment. I had a close-up look at its razor-sharp **claws**, thick *whiskers*, and amber **gold eyes**.

I was about to pass out when Trap shouted, "Get a hold of yourself, Germeister! How did you like my surprise? You're such a **scaredy-rat**! Can't you tell the mountain lion is fake?"

I reached out a trembling paw and gently touched the mountain lion. It was an enormouse **stuffed animal**!

Once my heart had stopped beating like a bongo drum, I lifted up the mountain lion and ran after Trap. **"When I catch you, I'll give you a mountain lion!"**

But Trap was too fast for me!

And thus, dear reader, ends this tale. Despite all my crazy misadventures, the Black Hills is one of my very favorite places. That **magnificent** piece of nature will always have a special place in my **heart**.

Good-bye, mouse friends, until the next adventure. It's sure to be a whisker-licking good one, or my name isn't *Geronimo Stilton*!

*I'm out of here!*

**#1 Lost Treasure of the Emerald Eye**

**#2 The Curse of the Cheese Pyramid**

**#3 Cat and Mouse in a Haunted House**

**#4 I'm Too Fond of My Fur!**

**#5 Four Mice Deep in the Jungle**

**#6 Paws Off, Cheddarface!**

**#7 Red Pizzas for a Blue Count**

**#8 Attack of the Bandit Cats**

**#9 A Fabumouse Vacation for Geronimo**

**#10 All Because of a Cup of Coffee**

**#11 It's Halloween, You 'Fraidy Mouse!**

**#12 Merry Christmas, Geronimo!**

**#13 The Phantom of the Subway**

**#14 The Temple of the Ruby of Fire**

**#15 The Mona Mousa Code**

**#16 A Cheese-Colored Camper**

**#17 Watch Your Whiskers, Stilton!**

**#18 Shipwreck on the Pirate Islands**

**#19 My Name Is Stilton, Geronimo Stilton**

**#20 Surf's Up, Geronimo!**

**#21 The Wild, Wild West**

**#22 The Secret of Cacklefur Castle**

**A Christmas Tale**

**#23 Valentine's Day Disaster**

**#24 Field Trip to Niagara Falls**

**#25 The Search for Sunken Treasure**

**#26 The Mummy with No Name**

**#27 The Christmas Toy Factory**

**#28 Wedding Crasher**

**#29 Down and Out Down Under**

**#30 The Mouse Island Marathon**

**#31 The Mysterious Cheese Thief**

**Christmas Catastrophe**

**#32 Valley of the Giant Skeletons**

**#33 Geronimo and the Gold Medal Mystery**

**#34 Geronimo Stilton, Secret Agent**

**#35 A Very Merry Christmas**

**#36 Geronimo's Valentine**

**#37 The Race Across America**

**#38 A Fabumouse School Adventure**

**#39 Singing Sensation**

**#40 The Karate Mouse**

**#41 Mighty Mount Kilimanjaro**

**#42 The Peculiar Pumpkin Thief**

**#43 I'm Not a Supermouse!**

**#44 The Giant Diamond Robbery**

**#45 Save the White Whale!**

**#46 The Haunted Castle**

**#47 Run for the Hills, Geronimo!**

*And coming soon!*

**#48 The Mystery in Venice**

Don't miss these very special editions!

## THE KINGDOM OF FANTASY

## THE QUEST FOR PARADISE:
THE RETURN TO THE KINGDOM OF FANTASY

## THE AMAZING VOYAGE:
THE THIRD ADVENTURE IN THE KINGDOM OF FANTASY

**Be sure to check out these exciting Thea Sisters adventures:**

**THEA STILTON AND THE DRAGON'S CODE**

**THEA STILTON AND THE MOUNTAIN OF FIRE**

**THEA STILTON AND THE GHOST OF THE SHIPWRECK**

**THEA STILTON AND THE SECRET CITY**

**THEA STILTON AND THE MYSTERY IN PARIS**

**THEA STILTON AND THE CHERRY BLOSSOM ADVENTURE**

**THEA STILTON AND THE STAR CASTAWAYS**

**THEA STILTON: BIG TROUBLE IN THE BIG APPLE**

# Meet
# CREEPELLA VON CACKLEFUR

I, *Geronimo Stilton*, have a lot of mouse friends, but none as **spooky** as my friend CREEPELLA VON CACKLEFUR! She is an enchanting and MYSTERIOUS mouse with a pet bat named **Bitewing**. YIKES! I'm a real 'fraidy mouse, but even I think CREEPELLA and her family are AWFULLY fascinating. I can't wait for you to read all about CREEPELLA in these fa-mouse-ly funny and **spectacularly spooky** tales!

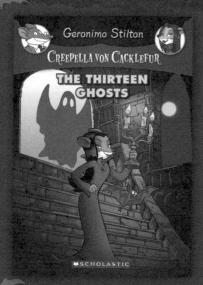

**#1 THE THIRTEEN GHOSTS**

**#2 MEET ME IN HORRORWOOD**

# ABOUT THE AUTHOR

Born in New Mouse City, Mouse Island, **GERONIMO STILTON** is Rattus Emeritus of Mousomorphic Literature and of Neo-Ratonic Comparative Philosophy. For the past twenty years, he has been running *The Rodent's Gazette*, New Mouse City's most widely read daily newspaper.

Stilton was awarded the Ratitzer Prize for his scoops on *The Curse of the Cheese Pyramid* and *The Search for Sunken Treasure*. He has also received the Andersen 2000 Prize for Personality of the Year. One of his bestsellers won the 2002 eBook Award for world's best ratlings' electronic book. His works have been published all over the globe.

In his spare time, Mr. Stilton collects antique cheese rinds and plays golf. But what he most enjoys is telling stories to his nephew Benjamin.

1. Main entrance
2. Printing presses (where the books and newspaper are printed)
3. Accounts department
4. Editorial room (where the editors, illustrators, and designers work)
5. Geronimo Stilton's office
6. Helicopter landing pad

*THE RODENT'S GAZETTE*

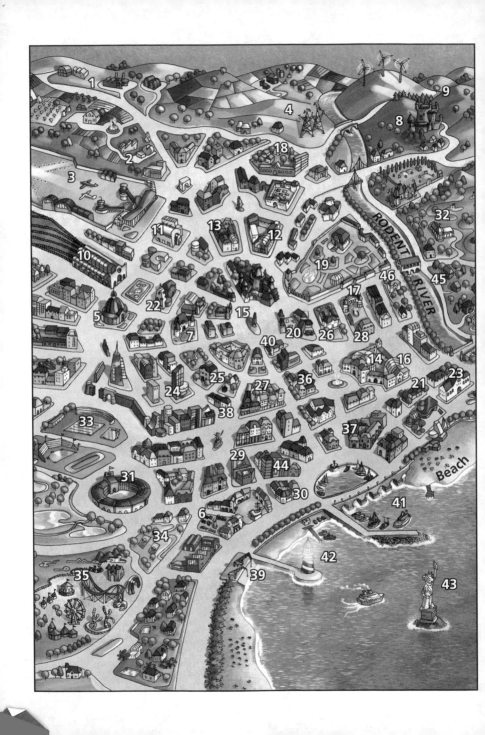

# Map of New Mouse City

1. Industrial Zone
2. Cheese Factories
3. Angorat International Airport
4. WRAT Radio and Television Station
5. Cheese Market
6. Fish Market
7. Town Hall
8. Snotnose Castle
9. The Seven Hills of Mouse Island
10. Mouse Central Station
11. Trade Center
12. Movie Theater
13. Gym
14. Catnegie Hall
15. Singing Stone Plaza
16. The Gouda Theater
17. Grand Hotel
18. Mouse General Hospital
19. Botanical Gardens
20. Cheap Junk for Less (Trap's store)
21. Parking Lot
22. Mouseum of Modern Art
23. University and Library
24. *The Daily Rat*
25. *The Rodent's Gazette*
26. Trap's House
27. Fashion District
28. The Mouse House Restaurant
29. Environmental Protection Center
30. Harbor Office
31. Mousidon Square Garden
32. Golf Course
33. Swimming Pool
34. Blushing Meadow Tennis Courts
35. Curlyfur Island Amusement Park
36. Geronimo's House
37. Historic District
38. Public Library
39. Shipyard
40. Thea's House
41. New Mouse Harbor
42. Luna Lighthouse
43. The Statue of Liberty
44. Hercule Poirat's Office
45. Petunia Pretty Paws's House
46. Grandfather William's House

# Map of Mouse Island

Dear mouse friends,
Thanks for reading, and farewell
till the next book.
It'll be another whisker-licking-good
adventure, and that's a promise!

Geronimo Stilton